Please return this item on or before
date stamped below.
Fines will be charged for any overdue item.

Southwark Council

(Previous issues:)

2 9 JUN 2010	- 8 NOV 2011	
- 8 SEP 2010		
		1 9 NOV 2012
	- 3 FEB 2012	
		3 0 NOV 2012
3 0	2 7 MAR 2012	
2 4 FEB 2011		3 1 JAN 2013
	1 8 APR 2012	
		2 6 FEB 2013
2 2 MAR 2011		
1 1 MAY 2011	1 6 OCT 2012	0 8 APR 2013
1 0 AUG 2011		2 6 NOV 2017

Monkey and the Water Dragon was written in the sixteenth century in China, by Wu Ch'eng-en. It is the story of an amazing journey.

The goddess Kuan-Yin chooses Tripitaka to fetch the Buddhist scriptures from India and bring them safely back to China. As Tripitaka is a gentle scholar, and not very brave, Kuan-Yin gives him two servants to protect him – the headstrong, mischievous Monkey and the lazy, greedy Pigsy. At the end of a journey full of many dangerous adventures, they are both rewarded with positions of honour in the court of the Jade Emperor.

DUTTON/PUFFIN

Published by the Penguin Group
Penguin Books Ltd, 80 Strand, London WC2R 0RL, England
Penguin Putnam Inc., 375 Hudson Street, New York, New York 10014, USA
Penguin Books Australia Ltd, 250 Camberwell Road, Camberwell, Victoria 3124, Australia
Penguin Books Canada Ltd, 10 Alcorn Avenue, Toronto, Ontario, Canada M4V 3B2
Penguin Books (NZ) Ltd, Cnr Rosedale and Airborne Roads, Albany, Auckland, New Zealand
Penguin Books (South Africa) (Pty) Ltd, 24 Sturdee Avenue, Rosebank 2196, South Africa

Penguin Books Ltd, Registered Offices: 80 Strand, London WC2R 0RL, England

www.penguin.com

First published by Dutton 1995
1 3 5 7 9 10 8 6 4 2

Published in Puffin Books 1997

Filmset in Monotype Baskerville

Made and printed in Italy by Printer Trento Srl

British Library Cataloguing in Publication Data
A CIP catalogue record for this book is available from the British Library

ISBN 0–525–69049–2 Hardback
ISBN 0–140–38417–0 Paperback

FOLK TALES OF THE WORLD

A FOLK TALE FROM CHINA

MONKEY AND THE WATER DRAGON

JOANNA TROUGHTON

DUTTON

PUFFIN

One day Tripitaka, Monkey and Pigsy came to a deep, wide river.

"We will never get across!" moaned Tripitaka. "It is too deep to wade and too wide to swim." He sat down and began to cry.

Monkey saw an old man and two
children at the river's edge. "Can you lend
us a boat to get across this river?" he asked.

"Do not come any nearer," warned the old man. "A terrible dragon lives in this river. Once a year he demands two children for his supper. This year it is the turn of my grandchildren. If we don't do as he wishes, the dragon will come out of the water and destroy the whole village!"

"This dragon won't be eating any more children!" declared Monkey. "He shall taste my cudgel instead!" Quickly he and Pigsy disguised themselves as the two grandchildren. "He will not know the difference," said Monkey.

Suddenly there was a horrible gurgling noise . . .

. . . and a huge dragon rose out of the water.

"Who shall I eat first?" he roared.
Monkey and Pigsy drew their weapons.
"No more children for your supper!" cried
Monkey. "Stand and fight!"
But the dragon gave a howl of anger and sank
beneath the water.

The dragon returned to his palace, deep down in the river.
"What's the matter?" asked a fish mother.
"I have been tricked out of my special supper," said the
dragon.

The fish mother had been looking forward to the supper too, for she always had a few titbits from the dragon's plate. She had a plan.

"Make a great snowstorm and freeze the river over," said the fish mother. "When Monkey and his friends try to cross it, you can crack the ice and seize them."

The next day, when Tripitaka, Monkey and Pigsy awoke, they saw that there had been a great snowstorm.

"Look!" exclaimed Tripitaka happily. "The river is frozen solid. Now we can cross safely to the other side."

But they had gone only a little way, when a huge hole appeared in the ice. Monkey and Pigsy used their magic powers and jumped into the air. But Tripitaka fell through the hole, deep down into the river.

Monkey turned himself into a crab and jumped into the river too. He found himself in an underwater palace, which was guarded by fish soldiers. In a corner of the palace there was a stone chest, and from the chest came the sound of someone crying. It was Tripitaka. "Do not cry, Master," whispered Monkey. "We will get you out . . . somehow!"

Monkey swam back to the shore. "I am not at my best in the water," he said to Pigsy. "You lure the dragon to the surface. Then I can deal with him."

So Pigsy dived down. "Water Dragon!" he cried. "You have trapped our master with an evil trick. Give him back to us at once, or you will feel my rake!"

The dragon rushed out with all his fish soldiers. "Your master is mine now!" he cried. "And no pig with a muck-rake is going to take him from me."

Pigsy quickly jumped out of the water and on to dry land, where Monkey was waiting.

"Look out for my cudgel!" cried Monkey, and he aimed a blow at the dragon's head. "Missed!" said Monkey, and the dragon disappeared beneath the water.

"This is no use," said Monkey. "I need help." He jumped on a cloud and travelled over land and sea, until he came to the palace of the goddess Kuan-Yin.

But Kuan-Yin was busy and Monkey had to wait. She was making a basket out of bamboo. What is the use of a bamboo basket? thought Monkey.

Monkey got tired of waiting. "Tripitaka is in great danger," he said.

"I know," said Kuan-Yin. She took up her basket, and she and Monkey travelled back to the great river.

Kuan-Yin lowered her basket into the water. She whispered some magic words that Monkey could not hear. When she lifted up her basket, there inside was a golden fish. "Here is your Water Dragon," she said.

"This golden fish once lived in my lotus pond. Every day it used to listen to me and the other goddesses as we talked of many things. This way it gained great wisdom and magical powers.

"One day a flood came. The golden fish was washed out of my pond and into the sea. So it came to this river, where it changed itself into a dragon and used its power in an evil way. Now go and free Tripitaka, and I will take my fish back to its pond, where it will do no more harm."

Monkey dived down and set Tripitaka free.

"We still have to cross the river," said Tripitaka.

"I can help," said a turtle. "The underwater palace was once mine, until the dragon and his fish soldiers drove me out. Thanks to your friends, the Water Dragon is gone. So let me carry you across the river on my back."

"This turtle's back looks very wobbly," said Tripitaka nervously.

"Don't worry," said the turtle. "I shall swim smoothly."
So the turtle took Tripitaka, Monkey and Pigsy safely
over the river to the other side. And if you do not know
how far they still had to travel, and whether other
dangers still awaited them, you must listen to what is told
in another story at another time.

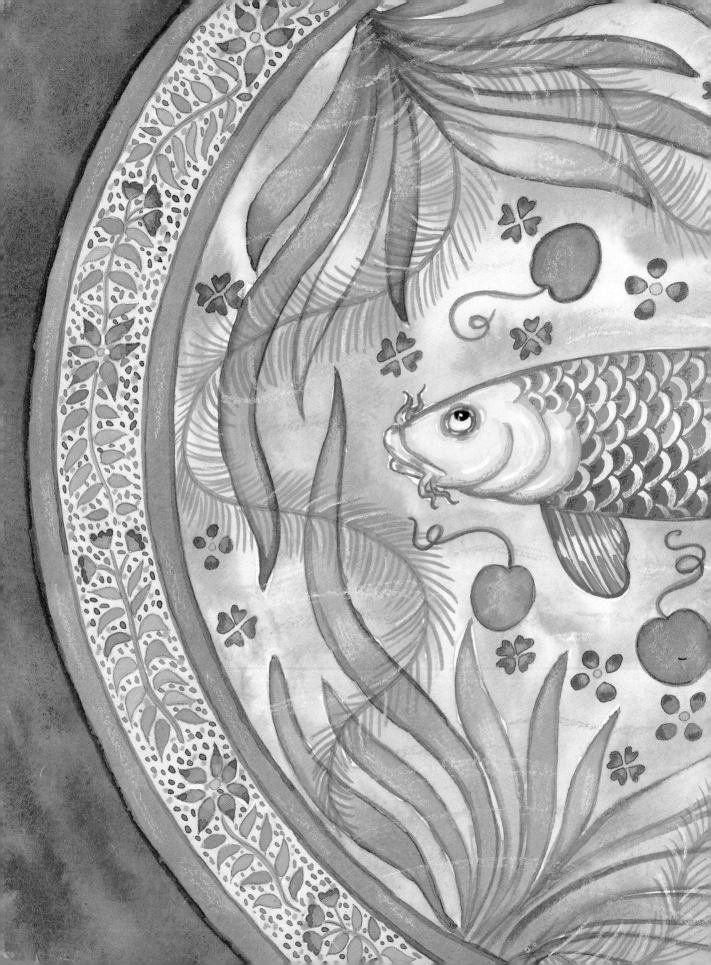